For Holly, Finley and
all those who believe
in magic
x

First published in 2016 by Big Little Toys Limited
Copyright © Big Little Toys Limited 2016.
All rights reserved.

Big Little Toys Limited, Portland House,
Belmont Business Park,
Durham, DH1 1TW
www.biglittletoys.com

ISBN 978-0-9954866-0-7

A catalogue copy of this book is available from the British Library.

Printed in the UK

FSC
www.fsc.org
MIX
Paper from
responsible sources
FSC® C013417

www.elfforchristmas.co.uk

Elf's First ADVENTURE

Written by Sarah Greenwell
and
Illustrated by Gillian Gamble

Published by Big Little Toys Limited

A little Elf was out exploring,
On a snowy evening stroll,
Admiring the fairy tale scenery,
At the faraway North Pole.

All of Santa's other elves,
Visited children far and wide,
But our little Elf felt lonely.
"What about me?" he cried.

Now Santa Claus had noticed
Little Elf was feeling sad.
"What can I do to make him smile?
It can't be all that bad!"

"I know!" thought Santa to himself,
"How to make our Elf feel better.
I'll give him some exciting jobs,
I'll write them in a letter!"

Elf read the note from Santa Claus,
He smiled from ear to ear.
His kind words made Elf feel happy,
And pleased that he was here.

"Please put stripes on the candy canes,
All of them red and white.
Wrap ribbons round the parcels too,
To make them nice and bright!"

"Next you can help my reindeer,
And teach them all to fly.
Please knit the snowman a hat and scarf,
To keep him warm and dry!"

Elf sailed through all his Christmas jobs,
And as soon as they were done,
"That's it!" thought Elf, feeling excited,
"I'm off to have some fun!"

Elf left his home at bedtime,
Soaring through the dark night sky.
Like a twinkling star, he flew past the moon.
He was up, so very high.

Suddenly Elf's ears pricked up,
At the snoring of a little girl and boy,
Finally, he'd found a family,
And it filled his heart with joy!

All at once the girl woke up,
The little boy did too.
"Nice to meet you," said little Elf.
"How do you do?"

"What on earth!" exclaimed the girl.
"You've landed in our house!
Small visitors are rare round here,
Though we did once have a mouse!"

Elf looked around their cosy home,
His eyes they filled with glee.
"Perhaps I can just stay a while,
Perhaps you will love me?"

Elf settled down to stay until Christmas,
He would bring kindness and fun.
But most importantly, while Elf was staying,
A special job had to be done.

Nice List
candidate

You are so much fun and well
behaved. Santa is going to make
your Christmas really special!

Little Elf watched all behaviour,
To prepare for Santa's Nice List.
It was a very big and important job.
No-one could be missed!

HOME,
SWEET HOME.

Elf flew back to Santa with a nightly report,
The children are doing so well.
But most of all, they are being kind,
And that is what Elf shall tell.

Elf did all sorts; spreading magic and fun,
The days were never dull.
The children played together nicely,
So their stockings would be full.

The children thanked their little friend,
For all that he had done.
"You're such a lovely caring Elf
You have been so much fun!"

"Aw really!" said the little Elf,
"You flatter me, you really, truly do!
My motto is: If you're kind to others,
Then they'll be kind to you!"

On Christmas Eve, around the world,
Excitement was under way.
Little Elf flew to the North Pole,
To prepare for Christmas Day.

Hurray! Our little Elf had succeeded,
His mission was all done.
Santa's sleigh was packed that night,
With gifts for everyone!

So please remember, it's so important,
That whatever you may do,
If it's nearly Christmas, please be good.
Elf has his eye on you!

Welcome to the North Pole

North Pole
Mail Room

Toy Workshop

Mrs Claus' Kitchen

Candy
Cane
Field

Enjoy more magical festive fun with Elf for Christmas

Welcome your own magical Christmas Elf straight from the
North Pole. Enjoy letters from Santa, reward charts, stickers,
report cards, Nice List certificates and more!

Grown ups - visit www.elfforchristmas.co.uk

Who will make it to the Nice List?

Magical activities, colouring sheets and more Elf fun is
available at www.elfforchristmas.co.uk